Brightly Coloured Horses

Brightly Coloured Horses

Mandy Huggins

Chapeltown Books

British Library Cataloguing in Publication Data

A Record of this Publication is available from the British Library

ISBN 978-1-910542-19-4

This edition published 2018 by Chapeltown Books
Manchester, England

For Ron and Mabel, who taught me the importance of kindness, stories, travel and good wine.

Contents

'There are only two or three human stories, and they go on repeating themselves as fiercely as if they had never happened before' – Willa Cather

Flight Path

Beyond the pier I watch two men as they repaint the end wall of the new apartment block a startling orange.

'It's the geese,' explains a voice behind me. 'The block has been built in their established flight path. On a dull day, or in the half-light of dusk, the geese think the grey wall is sky, and they fly into it.'

I know that it's you without turning round.

I have replayed that winter evening a hundred times. A goose had landed on the bridge, stunned after clipping a streetlight. As the skein flew on down the river, it staggered, bewildered, caged in by railings and relentless traffic. It had no runway.

You walked towards me and our eyes met. Without a word you took off your coat and threw it over the bird. We lifted it swiftly to the top of the railing, held it steady for only a moment, and then stood back. As it took off, its wings and underbelly were up-lit by the street lamps, aglimmer against the darkening sky. We smiled, suddenly a little awkward, and mumbled a few words before walking on.

Our flight paths momentarily crossed, our wing tips almost touched, but we did not collide. And since then I have thought of you often; my bird man. I have carried your voice in my head.

And when I turn I can see you have thought about me too. This time we will collide; even if to crash and burn.

The Last of Michiko

Every evening Hitoshi kneels on a blue cushion in the doorway that leads out to the garden. He leaves the *shoji* screens open regardless of the weather, and stays there until long after the sun has set. His heart knows that Michiko will never return, but his stubborn head finds reasons to postpone acceptance of the fact.

The wind chimes jingle softly through the house, as gentle as her voice, and in the sudden breeze they mimic her laugh. Hitoshi presses his face into a pink kimono, inhaling her faint scent. At his side stands a jar of her homemade adzuki bean paste, as sweet and red as her lips. He has rationed it carefully, but now this final jar is almost empty.

The day's post is propped up against the screen, and Hitoshi reaches for the bills and a letter from his daughter. She writes each week and always asks him to go and stay. Sometimes he thinks he will, but the trip to Tokyo seems like such a long journey now, and the city blinds him. There are no distances; everything is too densely packed, too close to see. And what about Michiko? He couldn't risk her returning in his absence.

His son lives nearer, but when Hitoshi sees the car pull up he stays out of sight and doesn't answer the door. He is saving them from the words that neither can bear to say. His son was the last to see Michiko; he watched the dark water snatch her away as though she were a brittle twig. When Hitoshi imagines it he pictures her hair floating upwards like the darkest seaweed, her skin so pale it appears as blue as the sea.

And though he has tried not to, he blames his son for failing to save her.

Some evenings Hitoshi thinks he hears a faint knocking, but when he goes outside the narrow street is always empty. He peers into the darkness for a moment; remembering the clack of wooden *geta* on the cobbles, glimpsing the soft light of the lantern outside the noodle shop. He imagines the warmth inside; the kind face of Koko as she pours the sake, and his friend, Wada, sitting at the counter waiting to mull over the old days. But Hitoshi always goes back inside and sits alone again in the dark.

Tonight there is no knocking, but just after seven o'clock he hears the doorbell. When he opens the screen, his neighbour, the young widow Emiko, stands beneath the light cradling a jar in both hands.

'I found this in the cupboard, Hitoshi-san, the last of Michiko's bean paste.'

As he takes the jar, Hitoshi stumbles under the weight of its significance. He looks up at Emiko as she backs away, and when their eyes meet she pauses. He bows, and gestures her inside, apologising for his rudeness. She steps past him, her kimono sweeping the *tatami* like a new broom, and the wind chimes fall silent.

Whatever Speed She Dared

The rear lights of the cars ahead disappear one by one over the inky horizon. There are no approaching headlamps, and nothing behind her.

She could drive in whichever lane she wanted at whatever speed she dared. She could swerve from lane to lane, wind down the windows, blast out *Born to Run*.

But the black moors frown down, pressing in from either side. She's heard a rumour that the bodies of children lie buried in the sodden peat.

She shivers, and moves over to the outside lane, slowing to sixty until headlights appear in her rear view mirror again.

Nelson

The summer we met, I sat on the porch and watched the tarmac shimmer with mirages, conjuring Ged's shape out of the arid haze as I waited for him.

Mama stayed inside, out of the sun, standing at the window in her stained satin slip. Sometimes she walked from room to room, opening drawers and cupboards as though searching for something to help her make sense of the world. She was waiting for my father to come back even though she knew he never would.

Ged was like him. He didn't say much, and I never minded. He talked with his eyes and his hands, and I knew he loved me. When we moved in together, we left town and rented a house by the lake. We were happy, or so I thought.

But I'd never seen the mask of silent anger and self-loathing that darkened his face for weeks at a time. When he came home from the garage he would take a cold beer and sit at the kitchen table staring at the wall. We no longer went down to the shore or hung out with our friends along the boardwalk.

Then Nelson arrived. Ged wasn't fond of cats. But he took to this tiny stray with the missing eye; the other the same bright blue as his own. Nelson was our charm, and I prayed for us.

One afternoon we got caught in a downpour as we were gathering firewood, and we raced back to the house, laughing. It was a rare good day; Ged seemed happy.

I threw our muddy clothes in the washing machine whilst Ged heated some soup. We sat down to eat and I asked if he'd seen Nelson. The cat had been asleep by the stove when we walked in, but now he'd disappeared. It wasn't like him to go out in the rain.

Our eyes met and we both jumped up. Nelson was always climbing in the washer. I ran through to the kitchen and saw his tiny body turning with the clothes. I hit the stop button, but I couldn't bear to look through the glass again and see him limp and still. Ged crouched down and peered into the drum.

'It's ok,' he said, 'he's still moving.'

We wrapped him in a towel and he fell asleep in the crook of Ged's arm.

Later, we made love for the first time in months. The rain had stopped, and through the open window I heard an owl. Nelson's tiny head lifted for a moment before he curled round asleep again.

I watched their faces as they slept. We were all safe.

But the next day Ged's eyes looked through me. I made pancakes for breakfast, but he said he was going into town. Nelson slipped out of the door behind him.

I stood at the window like my mother used to do, and waited for them both to come back. But neither of them ever did.

Your Own Children

Every August I see my summer boy on the beach. I have watched him grow up from my window. Sometimes I make sketches of him. A boy in Rory's image; caramel-skinned and lathe-thin, like a shaft of sunlight.

I saw him today, crouched over a rock pool, slender fingers entwined with the blood red tentacles of sea anemones. His bucket was full of iridescent shells and polished pebbles that would fade to pale as they dried.

I always wished the summer boy was Rory. I wanted to walk down to Balducci's with him for ice cream sodas, and then later, to varnish his pebbles so that they stayed forever bright.

Before he was anything else, Rory was your reassurance that you wouldn't let me down, that you'd finally tell your wife. He was wrapped in the shopping bag with my new skin-tight jeans, the ones I bought on the day we did the test, the ones I felt so good in. He was in my nervous laugh when I threw the bag across the bed and you pointed out that I may soon be too big for them.

At that moment Rory became the future: just me, a baby, and a life filled with bottles and nappies. And occasionally there'd be you. But in that vision the sea was always rough, and I couldn't see the horizon for rain on the glass.

Then Rory was my forehead against the cool bathroom tiles, and the knot in my stomach whilst I waited for the line to turn blue.

And, just like that, he was gone. Gone without touching the sides. Rory wasn't a blue line on a pregnancy test. He was a line missing. He was your obvious relief, your pale smile, your cold fingers on my arm. He was your voice telling me how you would have always been torn between this new baby and your own children. An odd thing to say: *your own children*. As though Rory would have been less yours in some way.

As I lay awake that night, my relief changed to grief. I mourned the loss of you and me, and the child that I hadn't wanted, but who was already formed in my mind.

In the morning we woke to an altered state, an imperceptible shift, the re-appraisal of an affair that had become something too weighty for us to lift. We had both glimpsed how the other would be, and we could never un-see it.

The next day you went back to being the good husband, and I went back to being the single girl.

Now I see you once a year, when you open up the cottage for those few precious weeks in August. And you bring me my summer boy.

Because all along you had your own Rory, already formed, already growing, already more than a blue line. That last unplanned baby.

And when we meet on the beach path, and you say hello, I catch Rory's ghost in your eyes. And your wife looks puzzled, and automatically reaches for my summer boy's hand.

Perfect Word

I look out of the hall window at the snow-silent street, and remember my father's word for the glitter frosting that sparkles beneath the streetlights: crackledust. I've never been sure about that word. 'Snow doesn't crackle, snow crunches,' I used to tell him. He'd just smile.

I stand in the hallway, surrounded by the neatly packed boxes and bin liners containing my father's clothes. I performed the task of sorting through them accompanied by a bottle of wine, packing systematically and methodically, without pause for the thoughts and memories that would have made it impossible. Jumpers, trousers, belts, shirts, ties; all neatly folded and coiled.

At the bottom of the banister is his green cardigan, the one with a hole in the sleeve and the leather buttons. I'm so used to seeing it there that I must have overlooked it earlier. My father had given that a made-up name too: swabbler. The cardigan that he wore for relaxing. For swabbling. I think it's a lovely word. I wrap it around my shoulders and open the front door to greet the silent early-hours world.

The snow is falling faster now. I throw my head back to catch the soft, fat flakes, and they melt like communion wafers on my tongue. I refused to take communion after the funeral, it would have been a sham, even though it was what my father had believed in. The body of Christ can't save me, only the blood of Christ: the wine that I drink to lessen the unexpected weight of grief.

As I stand in the garden I realise that although this house will always be my childhood home, soon it will belong to someone else, and I will never visit it again. I will never eat a whole plate of my mother's Yorkshire puddings filled with my father's onion gravy. I will never be late for my train because of the dining room clock that is permanently twelve minutes slow.

So do I now need my own word for lamp-lit snow? As it glints beneath the lights, a dusting of kali glitter, it's suddenly clear that I don't. I already have the perfect word. I wrap my father's cardigan tightly around myself and brush away tears with the rough wool sleeves. My childhood home isn't bricks and mortar; it's crackledust.

Junk

A small tow-haired boy shrieks with delight as he races towards the sea. He zigzags down the crowded beach, his legs like toothpicks in baggy blue shorts.

I want to watch him scramble between rock pools; parting fronds of seaweed to reveal starfish and tiny crabs. I want him to feel the silky softness of a donkey's ear squeezed between chocolatey fingers, and taste the sweet crunch of his first wafer cornet.

His mother leans heavily on the railings, the nub-end of a cigarette nipped tightly between thin lips. She flicks it across the pavement, yelling at him as he disappears down the beach. A voice to topple sandcastles; rasping the sand into submission.

'Get back 'ere *now*, we're goin' for chips!'

He slithers to a halt and turns towards the direction of her voice, hope and excitement draining from his face. He glances at the sea and then back up the beach, weighing the risks. She shouts again, and his skinny frame slumps in defeat.

As he walks back up to the road, she grabs his bucket of treasured shells and empties them onto the sand.

'And you can forget bringing that load o' junk wi' you 'n' all.'

My heart flips over, just like when the flight attendant announces the charity collection. I always know it's coming: the sentence that rips my heart out every time.

'Some of these children have never seen the sea.'

Waiting for the Rains

The monsoon is late this year.

I climb the stairs to the bar, where the ceiling fan labours pointlessly in the thick air, coating me with the slippery skin of the afternoon. I sit on the balcony at my usual table, peeling wisps of damp hair from my forehead.

Amit looks up to the sky, always hoping for rain to dissolve the unbroken blue. He nods to me as he squeezes fresh limes into soda. He brings the jug to the table with a tall tumbler, and a new bottle of vodka, the seal still intact.

'I am thinking the rains must come today, Miss Eleanor,' he says.

I don't answer, but pour myself a glass of neat vodka, and ignore the soda.

Every year, sick of the dust and sick of myself, I pray for the monsoon to come. Then, sick of the rains, I ache for the soft warmth before the fierce heat, the smell of the damp earth, and the women working in the fields, bobbing like vivid flowers amongst the fledgling shoots.

But in three hours' time I will be on a plane, leaving India behind, and this heat will no longer concern me.

I put the bottle of vodka into my bag, next to the envelope containing my air ticket and the letter from Vinnie, my son; the long-hoped for, but never expected letter, offering salvation and a place to end my days. My proper place, it would seem, is on the mock-Tudor avenues of suburbia, within earshot of the tired drone of the M1.

I pick up my suitcase and go out into the street. Amit calls down to me from the balcony. 'Miss! Miss! There are clouds. I tell you, the rains are coming!'

I look up and see that it's true. Low clouds have gathered, and I can feel the hint of a breeze on my bare arm. As I reach the taxi stand the sky opens wide, spilling fat raindrops. The water runs in rivulets beneath my feet, turning the red dust to mud. I open the car door and put my suitcase on the seat.

'Airport, miss?'

I tell him to wait a moment, and take the vodka out of my handbag, thrusting it into a nearby bag of rubbish. I look down at my shoes, caked with rich earth, and see the rain dancing on every surface, dripping from leaves like molten glass. It hammers on the corrugated rooves: ding-ting-ding-ting. Every year the rain saves me from myself, from self-pity and despair, and rinses out my fear.

I go over to the taxi and take my suitcase from the back seat. 'Sorry,' I say to the driver. 'Mistake.'

I retrieve the vodka, pushing Vinnie's letter into the bag in its place. Then I lay down in the road; a rain-starved flower, my limbs thrown wide in welcome.

Flask

Janey walked past the shelter where the tramp always sat. He was there even in the bitter cold. As always, she pretended not to see him, but as she climbed the icy path an idea came to her. She could bring him some of the homemade soup that was left over from last night.

When she came back out with her flask, snow was falling again. She could hear the soft sigh of the waves below, and through the trees she glimpsed the distant lights from fishing boats, marking the invisible horizon.

She grasped the frosty railing as she descended the slope, the wool of her glove sticking to the metal. For a moment she thought the tramp had gone, and part of her was relieved. But he was still there, huddled in the corner.

As she crossed the path she lost her footing, the flask crashed to the ground with her, and when she unscrewed the lid, the soup was a mess of glass. She considered turning round without saying anything. After all, it made no difference now.

But he called out to her, and asked if she was ok.

'I made you soup,' she said helplessly.

'Janey, isn't it?' he said. 'Don't worry, I don't expect you'll remember me.'

She shook her head. Maybe he knew her from the library.

The shelter was dank; names gouged into the bench. He had cardboard stuffed inside his coat, and a green hat pulled low over his ears. He held up a bottle of whisky, and laughed. 'This'll keep me warmer.'

Janey peered at him, trying to recognise a human face through beard and dirt. His eyes were dark. She had seen those eyes before, in another time.

'Here,' he said, offering the bottle, 'pour some into your flask cup.' He talked quietly, his voice raspy. There was something in the lilt that was almost familiar, perhaps altered beyond recognition by the roll-ups and the whisky.

As he lifted the bottle to his lips again, she noticed the tattoo on his hand. A faded rose at the base of his thumb. Her heart lurched, but she said nothing. Dave. Dave Spencer.

She saw his tanned chest, his arm flung above his head on the grass, his dark eyelashes resting on his cheek. Gently sleeping. Janey was only sixteen; he was only seventeen. She could smell the hot motorcycle engine, and see the shimmering road stretching ahead through that long summer. Her cowboy.

She handed him the flask cup. 'Keep it,' she said. 'I've got to go.'

Had she been just one girl amongst many? Did Dave Spencer even know that Janey had once loved him with all the madness in her teenage heart? She suddenly needed him to know, more than she needed to breathe. She walked over and kissed him. His lips tasted sweet and his eyes burned dangerously bright. As she climbed the path, she didn't turn round, but they both knew she would be back.

The Dung Beetle Race

In the midday sun, a skinny cat toys with her lunch: a dusty fish thrown down by the cafe owner. Eventually she settles under the table to eat, whilst fat black beetles hover like helicopters, their shiny bodies as thick as thumbs.

I think of the dung beetles we watched on the donkey track that day. They toiled in the shade of the olive groves, two of them, neck and neck, pursuing each other up the hill. You claimed your champion; the larger of the two, and named him Mr Turtle.

They stood on tiptoe, pushing their smooth golf balls of dung in a laboured race to the top. The balls juddered along the path, stumbling against small stones, stuttering to a near-halt as they adhered to fallen flowers and nubs of twig. Occasionally one of the beetles would stagger sideways. The ball would lose momentum and roll back an inch.

You laid a thin stalk of dry grass across the path: the finish line.

One of them spurted ahead. He nearly made the stalk, and then stopped. He waited for his race mate, giving him a chance, and only as he drew level did he set off again. Their balls touched the finish line in unison.

You turned to me then and asked if I would wait for you. You would be back here in one year's time. We would walk up the donkey track again, side by side, serenaded by cicadas.

I believed you, but you did not return. I should have seen that you were a cat, not a beetle, and I was simply your plaything in the dust.

Only the Best

From the shop doorway Deepal could see Aunt Sonia approaching. Her wide frame was perched precariously on the narrow seat of Amit's rickshaw. He weaved his way slowly through the top-heavy handcarts and piles of cooking pots that spilled out onto the street. Sonia stepped down, encased in cerise and emerald green, clutching a beribboned box to her chest as she picked her way through a pile of rotting mangoes.

'Namaste!'

Deepal pressed her hands together and bowed, then held aside the bead curtain to let her aunt into the two-roomed house tucked away behind the electrical shop.

'Lassi, Aunty-ji? You must be very hot?'

Deepal flicked the switch on the wall-mounted fan, and took out the lassi jug from the small refrigerator.

'Well, where is he then?' asked Sonia, gesturing around the room with her hands as though she expected the baby to be hidden somewhere.

'My mother has him today,' answered Deepal. 'She's taken him to visit Aunt Noosh.'

Sonia placed herself firmly on the only comfortable chair and held out the box to Deepal with one hand as she accepted her lassi with the other.

'Oh, such a shame! I wanted to see the child's face when you opened his present for him. But you can look anyway.'

Deepal thanked her aunt and unfastened the box, her heart already heavy. The box was from an expensive store in New Delhi, and she knew it would be something totally unsuitable; something she'd be unable to trade for nappies or clothes.

Nestled in tissue paper were a pair of tiny blue baby shoes. They were the softest leather, hand-stitched, with suede soles and velvet ribbons.

'Beautiful,' she exclaimed. 'Thank you so much, Aunty-ji!'

'Oh it's nothing! Only the best for my nephew.'

As soon as Sonia left, Deepal packed up the shoes and shouted for Vinod from the shop next door.

'Vinod, will your brother take these? Look at the label – they're from Italy.'

Vinod sucked his breath between his teeth and shook his head slowly.

'These are useless!' he said. 'Who would want such shoes? I'll give you Rs200 for them now, or you can wait until they are sold and take your cut. Usual terms.'

Rs200 was tempting; Deepal needed the money now. But the shoes were worth so much more.

'Ok, give me the Rs200. Take them before my husband knows I ever had them.'

The following morning the shoes were displayed in the window of Tanak's Emporium, with a handwritten sign declaring their superior Italian quality.

Deepal's husband saw them on his way home from work. He didn't usually notice things like baby shoes, but these were something special. Sure, they couldn't afford them, but they would make his wife so happy. And why not? Only the best for their baby.

He knew he was good for credit at Tanak's, and without hesitation he went inside. He couldn't wait to see Deepal's face when she opened the box.

To Be the Beach

At the end of the track a row of caravans came into view; four bleak hulks crouched in the grass-covered dunes. The one they stopped in front of was the dirtiest of them all: dented and rusty, coated with the salty skin of the seaside. A dead rabbit lay outside the door, flattened and bloodied, staring up at them through a single glassy eye. Lydia walked to the edge of the low cliff, where a few stunted trees still clung to the eroded bank. The sand below was littered with thick ropes of seaweed, broken shells, and dead starfish that had been caught out by the tide. The sea was grey and silent; far out at low ebb.

Without waiting for Dean she scrambled down the cliff path to the water's edge and stared out towards the horizon and the distant fishing boats.

Lydia wanted to be the beach; her wrinkles smoothed by the sea, her slate wiped clean, her rubbish swept away. The beach presented herself anew each morning, as though nothing had ever happened there before. As though no dog had ever raced headlong after a ball, leaving untidy paw prints in a skittering arc. As if lovers had never walked arm in arm along the shoreline, stooping to pick up shells.

She must leave Dean; she knew that. She must wipe clean the marks of his knuckles and his words. On the drive over she had almost believed this break would do them good; that he really meant what he said this time. When she looked down at the bruises on her wrists he had stroked her hand, switching on his familiar, lazy smile. But the damp caravan and the scowling sea made everything unbearable again. When she saw Dean kick the rabbit away with a vicious flick, Lydia knew it wasn't safe to stay.

A lone gull wheeled overhead, the bird's eerie cry mingling with Dean's voice as he shouted down to her from the cliff top. She turned with a start, automatically lifting her hand to wave. As she looked up she saw a red helium balloon. It jerked and dived and soared, pulling free, higher and higher, carrying a handwritten message to the world on its fluttering label. Perhaps a child was watching its steady climb from farther along the cliff top, waiting for the moment it disappeared into the sullen clouds: hope swallowed whole.

Dean called her name again, but she couldn't hear him anymore, she could only see his lips move. For a moment she allowed herself to imagine him slipping off the cliff edge and dashing his head against the jutting rocks.

Farther along the beach a dog was barking, and Lydia turned towards the sound. A collie raced in circles, waiting for his owner to throw a ball. The man's anorak was a splash of scarlet against the pale sand. He was her own bright, beckoning speck of hope.

Lydia set off slowly, then broke into a run.

The Turquoise Silk

My father strode into the bedroom, preceded by a rush of cool air from the corridor. He walked across to where my mother sat at the dressing table in her Nile green evening gown. He rested his hands on her shoulders for a moment, and their eyes met in the mirror.

'Don't be long darling, the car will be here in ten minutes.'

He ruffled my hair on his way out, eyeing my mother's pearls as I fastened them around my neck.

'Very glamorous, poppet. You be good for Nanny P, and put the light out when she tells you to.'

I nodded and smiled, inhaling his familiar sandalwood scent, but barely taking my eyes off my mother as she swept her hair into a tortoiseshell clip. This was always our special time, when I would sit cross-legged on the bed in my nightdress and watch her get ready. Her cream leather jewellery box was open in front of me, and I ran my fingers over the glittering tangle of diamante bracelets, necklaces of tiny iridescent shells, and cocktail rings set with rubies, amethysts, topaz, and amber.

I tried on the daisy clip earrings that always pinched my ears, and the ivory bracelets that slipped off my thin wrists, before re-examining each of my mother's evening bags, stroking the soft velvet pleats and the oyster silk linings, opening and closing the tiny jewelled clasps. There was always the hope of finding a leftover treasure inside; a lawn handkerchief stained with a lipstick kiss, or a ticket stub from the opera.

Then my mother asked the usual question.

'Which is it to be, darling?'

I handed her the green velvet bag, and held my breath as she twirled it in front of the mirror, before dangling it from her wrist by its slender chain.

'Good choice, sweetheart. Now let's get you tucked up in bed. You can read for half an hour.'

I woke up later to hear voices in the hallway below. My parents were back early because my mother was feeling faint. Crouched against the banisters, I watched my father carry her into the house, her bag still tangled around her wrist. I noticed straight away that it wasn't the green velvet, but the turquoise silk.

My mother had betrayed me.

When I cried, my father put his arm round me, assuring me that she would be well again before we knew it. He wasn't aware that she had betrayed me, or of everything that betrayal threw open to question.

After that night I didn't go up to my mother's bedroom to watch her get ready. Instead, I sat with Nanny P in the kitchen, drinking her special hot chocolate and watching our favourite game shows on the portable television. I only went upstairs after I'd heard the front door bang shut and the crunch of tyres on the gravel.

Brightly Coloured Horses

The man and the girl arrived at the Gare du Nord on a Friday evening. Anyone who cared to observe them would have thought them an odd match. Hugh melted into the crowd and left no lasting impression in his wake. He was blond like Marielle, but they were two different kinds of pale. She was spun gold, radiating light, whereas he was a dull kind of fair, where hair, skin, and features blended into beige.

She strode ahead of him down the street, a bright bloom weaving through the crowds, leaving Hugh to carry her suitcase as he followed. She was scarcely aware that men stared at her, and although she knew that Hugh could not be considered handsome, it had never mattered.

The hotel he'd picked was a short walk from the station. The brochure showed a classic facade, an over-gilded rococo lounge, and an old-fashioned lift with iron gates. But the room they were given was small, dark and womb-like, decorated in a deep crimson. The windows opened onto a crumbling balcony strewn with cigarette ends.

Marielle tried to hide her disappointment, but she'd looked forward to this visit to Paris for so long, and felt as though the hotel room was an inauspicious start. She ignored Hugh's suggestion they went to bed for an hour, and insisted instead that they freshened up and went straight out.

She said she was hungry, and they went back down the street to a bistro on the corner that offered a set price dinner. They ate inside, at a small booth in the window, and it was stuffy and warm despite the fact it was cool outside. The food was mediocre: the bread was yesterday's and their omelettes were overcooked. She smiled, and said it was fine, and they both drank too much wine because they knew it wasn't.

As they waited for their dessert they watched a woman feeding pigeons from a bag of bread and cake crumbs. A group of teenagers turned into the street and the birds took flight in a whir of wings. One of the girls picked up a larger piece of the bread and threw it at the woman's head. As she staggered sideways, the girl's friends laughed. Encouraged, she picked up another piece and swung her arm back again. Marielle looked at Hugh, but he just shrugged and muttered that it was none of their business.

Marielle leapt to her feet and ran outside, screeching at the group like a fishwife. They moved off, laughing, shouting in French that she didn't understand as they disappeared down the street.

She came back inside and sat down, suddenly aware that she was shaking.

Hugh hardly glanced at her. He was looking around the room to deflect the amused stares of their fellow diners. She didn't know what he was thinking, but she knew that something had changed between them. For some reason she had been sure he would be proud of her for intervening, for helping. But instead he seemed embarrassed by her, and she was sad that he was no longer on her side.

They said nothing to each other of this bleak discovery, but paid the bill and walked to the metro station to take a train for the Eiffel Tower, sitting in silence until they reached Champs de Mar. When they joined the queue for the tower, Marielle softened and took Hugh's arm, hoping it would be romantic when Paris was spread out beneath them in the dark, glittering like an open jewellery box.

But when they reached the platform it was crowded with tourists. There was loud chatter and cameras flashing in every direction. Marielle looked down at the view and Hugh reached for her hand. This wasn't how she'd imagined it. She thought he would take her outside and wrap his coat around her, enveloping the two of them in their own secret world. She had felt sure that this moment would save them, but it was too busy, too impersonal. Why had she thought that Paris would be anything other than a cliché?

When they came back down they walked over to the crepe stall by the merry-go-round. They bought coffee and sat down on a nearby bench. It was midnight. The carousel was closed but the music still played on, and the cleaner was sweeping between the brightly coloured horses, her hair tucked inside a flowered turban. The tower still sparkled with a million lights and the carousel was a riot of red and gold. It was Marielle's Parisienne moment; the thing she would always remember. But it would be her memory alone. They had moved to a place where they would always be side by side, seeing the same things differently, instead of watching for the reflection of a place in the other's smile. As she held the weight of this discovery, the finality became palpable to her, and it was a dull heavy thing.

The next day they queued to see the Mona Lisa and, like all of Paris, it was less than Marielle had hoped. She could scarcely see for the crowd that pressed behind her and around her; the painting was so small, so distanced by the glass surrounding it. She wanted to walk back and forth across the floor, to see the eyes follow her as they were famed to do. But the crowds closed in and they went back out into the sun.

She knew that Hugh would visit Paris again. He would take his wife and his daughters. They would go to a show, and he would watch dancing girls who – just for a moment – would make him think of Marielle. Then he would order champagne and chase her from his mind. And this would be how he would punish her, even though she wouldn't see it. He would do this until he had over-written the memories with something that made Paris good for him. But Marielle would still have her memory of the brightly coloured horses, and she didn't need Paris to be anything else.

They walked back through the streets side by side, both knowing that they had peeled back the dead layers of their affair and discovered its empty heart. They knew it was over, but each of them still said to the other how lovely it had been.

Warning Flag

The window blind was pulled halfway down, at an angle, as if hastily drawn against the midday sun. A hand reached for the catch and pushed the sash wide open. Two legs swung over the ledge, and two arms placed a basket of washing on the narrow balcony.

I could see it was Francesca. The sunlight caught her hair as she pegged out a blouse scattered with bright flowers.

It had been a year, but I was back, just as I had promised.

For a moment I wondered if I should climb the fire escape as I used to do. I had always tapped twice on the glass: it was our code. I remembered the jasmine scent of Francesca's warm skin. She would close her eyes, falling softly beneath me, pale limbs wrapped around pale limbs. Afterwards, still entwined, we would watch the sun slip behind the rooftops, and she would pour me a glass of ruby wine that changed colour with the sky.

Francesca leaned over the railing, shaking out a red silk scarf like a warning flag. For a moment I forgot to breathe.

And then she waved.

As I lifted my hand, a man brushed past me on the steps, calling Francesca's name. He kissed her, tilting her face up to him, and the red scarf fell from her hand, fluttering down to land at my feet. I picked up the damp silk square, already warmed by the sun, and pushed it into my pocket.

When I looked up again, the window blind was fully drawn.

The Mountain Cherry Blossom Corps

As Marnie walked through the door of the Imperial War Museum she reached for her boyfriend's hand. For a few minutes they moved silently around the vast space, glancing at the uniforms in glass cases, looking up at the fragile planes. The bombs unnerved her; even in their benign state their shape instinctively aroused fear.

She stopped at some photographs. Chilling images of a mushroom cloud; a bleak, broken wasteland; glass bottles melted into deformed shapes. Then she saw the plane. A single cherry blossom painted on its side. The young face of a pilot: Akito Watashi. Just seventeen years old, the same age as her. In his funeral portrait, he stared straight ahead. He had kind eyes.

Marnie squeezed her boyfriend's hand, but she didn't stop reading. *'The Yamazakura-tai – the Mountain Cherry Blossom Corps. Falling blossoms signifying death in battle. Eyes wide open in the face of the enemy. The battle cry: You and I are cherry blossoms in season…Every flower knows it must die. We will die gloriously, then, for our homeland.'*

She noticed a Japanese woman patiently waiting until they moved. They smiled at each other, and the woman bowed slightly as they swapped places in front of the display. As they walked away, Marnie saw her reach out towards the photograph of Akito Watashi and gently touch the glass with her finger.

When they stepped back out into the sunlight she walked quietly at Pete's side towards the trees. She understood that she must tell him now. It was there between them: a tangible thing, tiny, unacknowledged, barely formed.

'Pete?'

'Yes?'

She could see the future in his eyes, and knew that if she told him he would do the good, right thing. Marnie thought of the pilot with the kind eyes, about to sacrifice his life, and knew that she couldn't ask Pete to do the same.

'The museum was sad,' she said instead, and he kissed her hand.

As they walked away she saw the Japanese woman again. Their eyes met before the woman strode off into the weekend crowds. Marnie watched her disappear beyond the cherry trees. It was then that she saw the leaf; a single speck of pale green hope, taking its chance ahead of the blossom.

Without hesitation she turned to Pete and started again.

'Pete, there's something I must tell you.'

Twenty Dollar Shoes

The man's elbow digs into my ribcage, but I don't move. I need his tourist dollars. We're pressed together on the narrow bed in a mess of frowzy sheets, and his sagging flesh is clammy against my tanned skin. I turn to him with my paint-on smile and think of the good things. The yellow dress my sister is making for me, the matching shoes I'll buy later, and the certainty that one day I won't be in Havana. In America I'll have all the dresses I want, and a Cuban man who'll be kind to me.

And now the man is pressing down on me again, his sweat dripping onto my face, leaning in close to kiss me.

'Extra for kissing,' I say. 'Twenty dollars in total.'

I can get the yellow stilettos with twenty, and I know that with those shoes I can get the attention of the wealthy Americans, the older men who are here looking for the prettiest girls with the sweetest smiles. I need one of them to take me with him to Miami, and I know they won't take cheap corner hookers. When I get there I'll find a Cuban boy like Ernesto Angel, the only boy who ever cared about me.

And when he's finished, I wait patiently for his breathing to slow, for him to pull on his shorts and leave the money on the side.

He heaves himself up on one arm and looks at me.

'Twenty, you said?'

I nod as he reaches for his wallet.

Then he pauses.

'That's more than a whore like you's worth. But I'm feeling generous. Ten if you kick me out now, twenty if you let me stay longer – and we play to my rules.'

I think of the yellow shoes, the candy pink houses in Miami, and Ernesto's smile.

After he leaves I lie still. My wrists feel bruised, my lips swollen, and I can taste the metallic tang of blood. When I reach for the money it's just as I expect. There's only a single ten dollar bill pushed under the chipped statuette of Our Lady. Her watchful eyes reproach me and I turn her to face the wall. Then I get up and go through to the bathroom.

Everything will be ok. Tomorrow my sister will finish the yellow dress, and an American will fall in love with me.

About Life

The fields are crouched low, still striped with snow in every ridge, reluctant to thaw in the winter sunlight. You have just started ploughing. The first new furrows stretch away towards the cliff edge, dark and loamy.

I wave, but the sun reflects off the tractor windscreen, and I can't tell if you wave back. You reach the end of the field and circle. Now you have your back to me, your dark hair curling out from under your cap. I walk across the field and wait for you coming back down.

If I chose to, I could throw myself under the tractor at the last moment. I imagine the weight of the wheels forcing the breath out of me, pressing me down into the damp earth.

You wave now, but don't smile. I hold up the rucksack with your lunch. You reach the end of the field and stop, jump down from the cab and walk over to me. I hand over the flask of soup and the sandwiches. You bite into the thick bread and nod before walking back to the tractor, leaping up in one easy stride. I see you pour half a cup of soup, drink it quickly and screw the cap back on. Then you set off down the field.

I sit on the gate in the corner and eat my own sandwiches. I had hoped that you would stay and talk, like you used to do. But I should have known you wouldn't. My hands are cold without gloves, but I don't move. I watch you driving up and down the field, turning the earth; the seagulls swooping and diving overhead.

Everything you do is about life. Ploughing, planting, harvesting, tending new-born lambs and tiny yellow chicks that shudder into the world from fragile shells. Yet your shell has thickened. You prepare the earth for new life, but your own life is untilled and barren.

I set off across the field towards you. You see me and look away. We both know that if our eyes meet, the truth will rear up and slam into us like a concrete wall.

Our son is dead.

Blond curls camouflaged in the straw, pale limbs in a tangled sprawl beneath the sagging loft beam that finally gave way.

Mired in guilt we fire blame back and forth, meting out revenge in withheld smiles and frozen silence. You can no longer say my name, and I ache to hear it.

The wheels roll towards me and I can see your face clearly. There is a flash of fear in your eyes as I jump. You try to swerve. The tractor judders as the tyre glances my shoulder, and I lurch back, throwing myself to the ground. The engine stops, and for a moment there is only the murmur of the radio. Then I hear you clambering down, stumbling in your haste, and shouting my name.

Just for the Dance

When they left the bar, the snow was still falling. Alice threw her head back to catch the flakes, dizzy with the wine she had drunk to forget their debts and their doubts.

The world had been silenced by a quilt of snow, and beyond the car park the trees were stilled with its weight. Alice picked up a handful and fashioned a snowball, sliding in her high-heeled boots. It caught Carl on the back of the neck as he opened the door to the pickup. He looked puzzled for a moment, then a ghost of a smile played around his eyes.

They drove home slowly, the heater turned up high, and the snow falling softly against the windscreen. So white, everything so white, and in Alice's head everything still so dark. Carl sang along to the radio, his voice like a lullaby. The caramel voice of the DJ drifted over the start of the next song, and their eyes met. It was their song.

Carl stopped the truck, jumped down, opened the door for her and held out his hand. She caught the toe of her cowboy boot in the step and fell forward onto the solid weight of him, breathing in the woodsmoke scent of his sweater. He took her in his arms, and they danced in the light of their headlamps as the snow fell around them, flakes settling on their hair and shoulders like lace. Carl sang to her, and Alice smiled. The old smile, that Carl rarely saw; because she knew that nothing could ever be perfect, but sometimes it could be alright, even if it was just for a three-minute dance.

Blood Red

A small red ball sidled along the gutter, negotiated a flattened beer can, then gathered speed as it neared the drain. Walter bent to rescue it, then continued at his former pace, arriving at the office at exactly 8.55.

He opened the window, hung his coat behind the door, and examined the smooth texture of the ball for a moment, testing the weight of it in his hand.

There was no view from his tiny rear office, nothing to distract him from the routine of the day. It was the first hot morning of the summer, and he flicked the wall switch for the overhead fan. It creaked into action for a single revolution, sighed, and stopped. Walter threw the ball at the ceiling in frustration. It glanced off the fan blade and flew unnoticed out of the window, hitting the visor of a passing motorcycle courier.

A moment later, Walter heard the raw screech of brakes. He peered out over the ledge, but couldn't see to the end of the street. He shook his head and sat back down. After the wail of the ambulance siren had faded into the distance, Walter went to the kitchen to make his first coffee of the day. As he passed the sales office he heard shrieking, and then Amy Potter burst into the corridor and made for the kitchen ahead of him. As he walked in she was running the cold tap, a glass tumbler in her hand.

'Mr Patchett, have you the heard the dreadful news? Chloe Broadbent has been in an accident. Just now, on the way back from the bank. A motorcycle courier swerved into a car, and the car mounted the kerb and knocked her down. It's terrible!'

Her words tumbled out in a breathless rush, and Walter patted her on the arm. He wasn't very good in these situations, and now Amy was threatening tears.

'I'm sure she'll be fine.'

'No, Mr Patchett, you don't understand. Mr Dawes in purchasing saw it happen. He says she's dead!'

Walter flapped his arms uselessly for a moment, and then took the glass from Amy's shaking hand. The volume of the other girls' voices rose and fell as the sales office door opened and closed.

'You go back in the office and calm things down, I'll make everyone a cup of sweet tea.'

He tried to remember which of the girls was Chloe Broadbent. Was she the little blonde one? Or was that Lydia? No, he was sure Chloe was the blonde one. A nice girl. It was so frightening the way everything could change in a single moment, and all because of some fool's reckless driving.

Walter stopped at the kitchen window, kettle in hand, and glimpsed a small red ball coming to rest against the kerb below. Blood red. He turned to see a policewoman in the corridor, and gently pushed the door closed with his foot.

Fatal Flaw

I am sorry about today. But when I saw you, it was as though someone had punched me in the stomach. I was winded.

A chance encounter on a Sunday afternoon in London. What were the odds?

You didn't see me; you were too engrossed in your conversation with Max. You were laughing, and your head was thrown back, revealing your pale throat. An unguarded moment, where you left yourself vulnerable to the lions. Max pointed at something across the river, and you screwed your eyes up; as usual you weren't wearing your glasses. He nudged you with his shoulder and you both laughed.

I couldn't move towards you, and I couldn't walk away.

It was not the you I was used to seeing. I only ever see the once-a-year you, the you that shocks me anew every time with your passion; your shine always much brighter than I remember. It's as though, between our meetings, I can never hold on to the memory of you with enough intensity. I can never recall, until the moment I see you again, just how wide your smile is, or how velvet your skin.

And Max? He was a mistake. That's what you called it that night when we ran into each other at the theatre – a mistake. The night that we counted up the seven long years since we'd seen each other. The night we stayed in a cheap hotel room and you said you wished we were still together. I told you about Ruby, and I said that I'd made a mistake too. I don't even know if I really meant that – not then. But you bewitched me with your brightness, your subtle curves, your clarity. Everything about you soared.

There's nothing we can do, you said. And so we made a pact to meet just once a year.

I believed I had the essence of you; the best part. I rarely considered what you gave to Max, or the part of you that was his. I blocked out your other life, and I was sure that I knew the secret. I thought that if you were the woman I couldn't have then you'd stay the woman that always shone.

But when I saw you this afternoon, I realised that you and Max still shine for each other. Only this is a different shine. Because when you handle something every day it gains a patina, a depth of polish, far richer than the novelty of box-fresh. Even the fault lines and fissures become a part of the beauty; repaired with something more valuable than the original material.

But whatever else I got wrong, this I know to be true: no matter how strong your age-mellowed love may be, there is always the chance of a fatal flaw; the possibility of damage from which there can be no recovery.

So I walked over to you and introduced myself to Max.

Waiting

Sylvie leant heavily on two sticks, and watched her husband as he set out to the épicerie. He paused at the corner as always, and waved his hat before he turned and disappeared from view.

He knew that she wouldn't go back inside. She would lower herself onto the sun-bleached bench, and stay there, resting against the dusty wall, shaded by a cloud of bougainvillea, waiting patiently for him to return.

He doffed his hat to Madame Rousseau as he passed the hotel, remembering how all the village boys used to vie for her attention at the Saturday dance.

In the shop he flirted with Celine, and stopped for a quick glass of pastis with Henri. When he stood up to leave, the shadows of the cypress trees were lengthening.

He knew that his wife would still be waiting; the foolish old girl. She would be stood up again now, leant against the doorframe: silent, motionless, eyes fixed on the bend in the road, just as she had once waited for him to come back from the war. When he reappeared around the corner he would see her exhale; a whisper of a sigh, scarcely audible.

He carried a heavy cloth shopping bag in one hand and a long baguette was tucked under his other arm. When she came into view he carefully placed the bag down, before brandishing both the bread and his hat to signal that all was well.

She waved her arms and rolled her eyes as though she thought him an old fool.

As he drew closer he could see that a drift of pink petals had fallen onto her hair. And just as he always did, he pictured the soft bloom of her peachy skin when they first met; her body like a newly opened flower in the shade of the olive groves.

She took the shopping bag and fussed around him; talking, talking. He didn't listen to what she was saying. He rarely listened to her nonsense these days; he just agreed with an absent nod.

More and more often he found himself returning to that one perfect day in the olive groves. In all the eighty-seven years of his life she was the only thing that he had ever longed for that had been worth the wait.

Kisses

Kevin Healey's kisses tasted like dunked biscuits.

The first time he kissed me was at the scout hut dance, behind the stage curtains. It was Christmas, and the hall was decked with plastic mistletoe and dusty paper chains.

When Rosie and I danced to *Tiger Feet* Kevin Healey and his mate moved in to dance with us. Above our heads, the badly glued paper chains broke and fell around us in a tangle of red and green. It all seemed so romantic, and when the record finished Kevin took my hand and asked me over to the stage.

And now Kevin Healey is here in Tesco's. He's with a small girl looking at the Christmas decorations, and they're talking quietly about baubles and tinsel. I don't know how I recognise him; I don't recall seeing him since I was fourteen. His hair has darkened to a soft auburn, but his freckles are the same.

'Aren't you Kevin Healey?' I ask.

He turns round and looks at me. At first his face is a blank, but then he smiles.

'Julie Pearson?'

I laugh. 'Not totally changed beyond recognition then?'

He shakes his head. 'No, you're looking good.'

'Thanks,' I mutter, noticing that his little girl is staring at me rather oddly. I decide it's probably best to leave it right there, and I continue down the aisle with a little embarrassed wave.

What more was there to say to a man who you kissed a few times behind a faded green curtain? Except that I can remember those kisses more vividly than any others since, because the kisses themselves were the important thing. Not long after that, kisses became a part of something else. They were bit players in the opening scene of a greater passion, a walk on part in the opera of love-making.

But the kisses with Kevin were kisses for kisses' sake. Exploratory kisses. Kisses that were meant for tasting, for rolling around the mouth and savouring. They were kisses that simply led to more kisses. Kisses that made my mouth sore, kisses that made my tongue swell. Beautiful teenage kisses.

I turn round and look back at Kevin Healey. The girl is engrossed in picking out a fairy for the tree, and Kevin has walked further up the aisle in my direction.

Without thinking I turn towards him. I want to taste his mouth again, his sweet, malty, biscuity mouth. I take him by surprise as I lunge forward, and he staggers back a step into a woman who has walked up behind him.

'Kevin?' Her eyebrows are raised in a questioning manner as she looks me up and down.

'Er…Julie, this is my wife, Carol,' he says. 'Carol, this is Julie, an old school friend.'

I nod and smile, mutter my apologies and walk away, stopping briefly to pick up a box of old-fashioned paper chains before I head over to the biscuit aisle for a packet of rich tea.

The Remains of the Evening

Edie's tour group were gathering in the downstairs lobby before dinner. Her husband, Jack, was already there. She could picture them all, slightly self-conscious in their kimonos and house shoes, drinking their first beer a little too fast, and throwing their heads back in polite laughter as they swapped tales of their day's climb.

She tied her kimono sash tightly and pulled back the sliding paper screens. The mountains glowed pink in the dusk, and the air was cool. This was her favourite time of day.

Matsuo, the hotel manager, stood below her window, holding a thin cigarette between thumb and forefinger. He sensed her presence and looked up at the window, then bowed imperceptibly and turned back towards the door. Edie shivered, and felt an inexplicable yearning for all the alternative lives she would never lead.

Impulsively, she picked up her coat. She couldn't face another evening of pointless banter and one-upmanship. She'd take a walk, and try to turn the remains of the evening into something beautiful. She smiled at Matsuo as she passed his office door, and as she turned she noticed that the keys for the private outdoor *onsen* baths were both on their hooks. On impulse she grabbed one of the wooden fobs and headed outside. Jack would probably come looking for her, but she didn't care. All she wanted was to lower her body into the hot spring waters and gaze at the stars. She fumbled with the lock, and as the door swung open Matsuo caught up with her and handed her a towel. She thanked him.

'If anyone asks, please don't tell them where I am.'

'Hai.' Matsuo nodded, and stepped back as if to leave, but as she went through the doorway he slipped through with her. When her hand paused on the door handle he pushed it gently shut and turned the key.

He went into the shower hut, took off his clothes and placed them in a basket on the shelf. Edie turned away, and when she looked again he had unhooked the shower and started to wash.

She undressed, and walked over to the shower at the other side. After a few minutes she heard Matsuo turn off the taps and leave the hut. Edie waited a moment and then followed him outside, walking across to the farthest edge of the rocks before gently lowering herself into the water.

As she studied the curve of his shoulders through the wisps of steam, she was aware that he was watching her. When she met his gaze he closed his eyes, and they sat together, silent, in the warm cocoon of the water. The branch of a cherry tree hung over the high wall, and a soft breeze blew a single perfect blossom onto his hair; pale against the black.

Somewhere in the distance she could hear the sound of false laughter; but no one came to find her.

Shooting Stars

Miranda and Lionel travelled by ferry from Nice to Corsica, and found a tiny *bergerie* to rent in the northern mountains of La Balagne. It was high season and the woman in the tourist office told them that they were lucky to find anywhere.

Their only neighbour was a farmer, Jean-Luc, who lived in a house behind olive trees at the other side of the lane, and who introduced himself by bringing a gift of tomatoes and basil from his garden.

Miranda was happy to be here after the cosmopolitan chatter of the cafe life in Nice. Her husband had known many of the other guests at the Hotel Renee, and every night they had strolled along the Promenade des Anglais together and finished their evenings with brandy and coffee in the Cafe Jardin. The women's laughter was shrill and their conversation pointless.

She told Lionel that she felt more at home here in the mountains. He smiled and ruffled her hair and went back to reading his newspaper. He found it hard to relax, as he loved the company of his friends, and was not one for making his own entertainment. During the days he would drive Miranda along the narrow mountain roads in his open-top car. She would tie her long hair back with a blue ribbon, and they would go down to the coast for lunch, and watch the Italian tourists stroll by in their designer clothes.

And at night they would walk up to the village for an early dinner, and then sit outside the *bergerie* with their brandy as lizards darted around the lights.

Miranda would lay awake long after her husband had gone to sleep. She would think about all the men that she would never know. The men with rough hands and dark eyes, the men who cared nothing for expensive clothes or vacuous small talk. The men who would take her body without offering their love.

Sometimes Lionel would look at her as though she were a question that he didn't understand, but she knew that she had made the right choice. He was the man she had chosen to save her from herself; the man who would protect her from what she wanted.

And some nights Miranda would go out into the garden after Lionel had fallen asleep. She would walk barefoot so she could feel the dry grass under the soles of her feet, and wait for the shooting stars to arc across the darkness.

One afternoon they strolled up to the village earlier than usual for a drink before dinner. The sun threw long shadows across the deserted main street and they sat alone on the restaurant terrace with their cold beers. As the afternoon turned to dusk, Bartoli lit the pizza oven and called across to four villagers playing petanque, to ask if Lionel and Miranda could join the final game whilst they waited for their food. They took their places on opposite teams, and Miranda realised that one of her team was their neighbour, Jean-Luc. He bowed to her and kissed her hand, and she found herself blushing.

The village men came and sat at their table afterwards, and Bartoli translated the conversation from Corsican into basic French for them. Miranda drank too much wine and flirted openly, untying her hair and letting it hang loose in a waterfall of ripened wheat. Jean-Luc rested his arm along the back of her chair, and she leaned against it to feel the warmth of his skin against her bare shoulder. She imagined the taste of his lips and the feel of his rough workman's hands.

When Lionel asked her to leave with him she told him to go alone. But they only had one torch and he wouldn't go without her. She protested that Jean-Luc would walk her down later, but Lionel took her by the hand and pulled her to her feet. The village men all cheered and laughed as she staggered down the street, and she blew kisses at them.

And when she couldn't sleep she slipped out into the moonlight as always, and walked naked to the other side of the garden. She threw her head back and watched the shooting stars high above. And she didn't cry out when two strong arms encircled her from behind, because she knew who it was without turning round. She had been expecting him.

As she lay down in the grass, the earth was still warm beneath her, but she shivered as she looked into Jean-Luc's eyes.

Moonlight danced on the swimming pool, and the reflections that ran over their skin made it appear as though they were underwater. As their pale limbs tangled and arced, they rose and fell as one; they were sub-aqua shooting stars. She felt no guilt or doubt; this man made her feel part of the earth and the sky.

No one, not even Lionel, could protect her from what she wanted.

Car by Car

Marilyn was a curvaceous coupe, customised with gleaming chrome. She arrived on the heels of your rough-edged street girls: a shining temptress.

But I had fond memories of cruising along the seafront in your rust-stained Ford, lured by the lights that danced on the water.

Then there was the Triumph Stag with her retro elegance. After our wedding your friends tied beer cans to the exhaust, and we lost them one by one until all that remained was a tangle of ribbons.

The Volvo came next; the reluctant beast that needed a bump start every morning when you left for work. The car that saw me stood halfway down the street in my bathrobe, smiling as you waved through the sunroof.

Then Marilyn. The only car to be given a name. Marilyn was a bargain, you said, we'd be fools not to snap her up. And we soon found out why she was so cheap – whilst parked at the roadside she'd been written off by a drunk driver.

Perhaps she was jinxed, or maybe it was coincidence, but from the day you brought Marilyn home she was a witness to our meltdown, and her imperfect chassis became the emblem of our undoing.

You lost your job and started drinking, stayed out late and came home angry. You begged forgiveness and then did it all again. We were running on empty.

And then you told me you were in love with the waitress from the Tomato Dip. I broke down, and we broke up.

The weekend you left, I drove recklessly around the village, barefoot and drunk, until I crashed into the farm wall.

You let them tow Marilyn to the scrapyard, and just like all the other cars before her, she left with a tiny part of us still inside. The final part. Now we were a write off too.

The Right Castanets

One summer, when Sandy was ten or eleven years old, her parents rented a pale pink villa on the outskirts of a fishing village in Catalonia. Her mother took Spanish lessons before they went, but the maid always shrugged and frowned, and acted as though she hadn't understood her. Maria was raven-haired, and wore bright skirts and low-cut blouses. She had an earthy sensuality that made Sandy feel uneasy, and because she didn't understand her, she didn't like her.

They would sit at the large kitchen table every evening and eat olives and fresh anchovies whilst they watched Maria prepare their meal. Sandy's mother gave her money for the shopping every day, and she would bring back loaves of dense bread with thick dark crusts, cloth bags of rice, and iridescent fish straight from the quayside.

One evening they told Maria to take the night off, and drove inland up into the mountains. Sandy's parents had heard that there was a fiesta in the next town. They stopped en route at a village bodega. The inside was musty and cool after the heat of the day. Sandy and her mother sat at tables made from wine casks, whilst her father sat up at the bar and chatted to the barman. He was slim-hipped with dark, liquid eyes, and there was something about him that made Sandy blush when he smiled. When she went up to ask for another drink she tried to stay with her father at the bar, but he waved her away and told her to keep her mother company.

'The barman is called Juan,' she said as she sat back down. Her mother pursed her lips and told her she was too young to be thinking about the names of waiters.

When they arrived at the town the streets smelt of garlic and spicy sausage. The men were cooking huge pans of paella in the main square. Crimson-lipped women stood chatting in groups. They wore dresses splashed with bold polka dots, and had turquoise flowers pinned in their oiled hair. They seemed dangerous to Sandy; knowing and bold. Like Maria.

There was music playing in the streets, and laughter coming from the doorways of the bars and cafes. Sandy wanted to buy castanets from a street vendor. They were roughly carved and painted with pictures of toreadors and flamenco dancers, stained with a thick varnish and threaded together with coarse, coloured string.

Her father wouldn't let her buy them; he said they were asking an inflated price because of the fiesta, and that they would get her some the next day in the village.

But when Sandy held them in her hand she was disappointed. They were somehow all wrong. They were plastic, and the pictures were not painted on by hand, they were just transfers. But she knew that her father didn't know the difference, or think that it mattered. So she was grateful and said nothing.

She took them down to the beach and practised playing them until her mother lost her temper. But no matter how hard she tried she couldn't get them to sound like the ones she had heard at the fiesta. They sounded thin and cheap.

Eventually she went across to the villa for her lilo. Her father was already back there, enjoying an early siesta as he did every day.

The house was silent as she walked through the kitchen to the hallway. Then she heard a stifled cry and low voices. The sound was coming from her parents' room, and she carefully opened the door.

Juan, the barman from the bodega, was stood by the bed in his shorts. Both men were both facing away from her, but they heard the squeak of the door. Her father pushed Juan to one side and hastily pulled a crumpled sheet around his waist. He muttered something, and Juan turned towards her.

'Er... darling,' her father stuttered, 'Juan was just passing by, and I... I... asked him in for a drink. But then I knocked it all over him... and so... and so I'm lending him some clothes. No harm done – we don't need to tell your mother do we, sweetheart? You know how cross she gets.'

Sandy turned, confused, and rushed out into the corridor, slamming the door. As she raced to the kitchen, her father caught her up and grabbed her arm, his other hand clutching the sheet.

'We'll go to the shops later and I'll buy you something – one of those guitars you were looking at perhaps? What do you say, Sandy?'

She shook her head. 'I want the right castanets,' she said. 'The wooden ones with pictures of bullfighters and dancers.'

The next morning they went into town to buy them. She usually loved spending time on her own with her father, but today she wanted to be on the beach with her mother. He held her hand, but it felt clammy and she wriggled away, pretending to look in a shop window.

When her father handed over the money for the castanets, Sandy was reminded of what her mother always said when he arrived home late with a hastily bought bunch of roses.

'I can't be bought that cheaply, Lionel.'

When she opened the parcel they looked tacky. There were splinters of wood inside where they had not been sanded down properly, the varnish was hastily applied and had dried in drips, and the picture of the bullfighter reminded her of Juan and his flashing eyes. Yet she knew they were just the same as the ones she had coveted at the fiesta. Sandy felt let down, and disappointed, without fully understanding why.

She put them at the bottom of her drawer underneath her tee-shirts, and when they returned home she left them behind. They weren't the right castanets after all.

Previous Credits

Flight Path – Winner of the *Words with Jam* e-zine Shortest Story Competition 2014.

The Last of Michiko – Highly Commended in the *Bare Fiction Magazine* Flash Fiction Award 2015.

Nelson – Runner-up in the 2015 Multi-Story Flash Fiction Competition.

Your Own Children – a previous version of this story was runner up in the *Writers' Forum* Flash Fiction Competition 2014. It was also Commended in the Ink Tears 2015 competition.

Perfect Word – appeared in the English Pen *Dictionary of Made-Up Words* in 2013. It was also Commended in the Ink Tears Flash Fiction competition in 2013, and appeared on the *Stories for Homes* website.

Junk – won *The Yellow Room* Flash Fiction Competition in 2012 and appeared in *A Million Stories* anthology in 2015.

Waiting for the Rains – published in *Wherever You Roam: Slim Volume II* anthology in 2015.

Flask – appeared on the NFFD Flash Flood Journal website in 2015

The Dung Beetle Race – won 5th place in *The Yellow Room* Flash Fiction Competition 2012.

Only the Best – appeared in the *For Sale: Baby Shoes, Never Worn* anthology 2017.

To Be the Beach – Winner of the Retreat West Quarterly Flash Fiction Competition 2017.

The Mountain Cherry Blossom Corps – Highly Commended in the 2016 Ink Tears Flash Fiction Competition.

About Life – won 3rd place in *The Yellow Room* Flash Fiction Competition in 2013.

Just for the Dance – a shorter version of this story was commended in the *Reader's Digest* 100 Word Competition in 2014.

Blood Red – appeared in the 'Kill People' edition of the *Jellyfish Review* in 2017.

Fatal Flaw – won 2nd place in the Word Hut Competition 2014.

Kisses – a previous version of this story won the Write Invite Competition in December 2012.

Car by Car – previously appeared on the Reflex Fiction website 2017.

Shooting Stars – won 3rd prize in *The Yellow Room* short story competition 2012.

Praise for stories in *Brightly Coloured Horses*

Nelson – 'Superbly written: lean, vivid, constantly painting a picture. Beautifully observed, touching and...oh so true.' – John Goldsmith, author and Emmy-nominated screenwriter.

Flight Path – 'This tiny love story about an unexpected connection with a stranger layers sparse prose with carefully coordinated detail. I felt as if I'd read a painting, as much as a story.' – Debbie Young, author of *Best Murder in Show*.

Waiting for the Rains – 'A beautiful expose of the disillusioned expat. The main character is buffeted by her own fears and confusion as to where she should be in her later years. In the end the rains decide for her.' – Vic Errington, Multi Story

Only the Best – '...is utterly charming. I didn't see the end coming at all and I just love it.' – Hache Jones, Editor of *For Sale: Baby Shoes, Never Worn*

Twenty Dollar Shoes – 'This story is raw and uncompromising, dealing with one woman's brave mission to escape the grinding poverty of her life. I thought of Tina Turner's amazing Private Dancer, and there were also echoes of John Steinbeck at his gritty best.' – Fiona Cooper, author.

About Life – '...this writer has a wonderful feel for language. Her characters leap off the page...' – Jo Derrick, award-winning writer and former Editor of *The Yellow Room*.

Also By Chapeltown Books

Spectrum
by Christopher Bowles

A collection of one hundred and ten pieces of flash-fiction and poetry. You probably won't like all of them, and some of them might even disgust you, or make you uncomfortable. But stick with it. Look at overarching themes within each coloured block. Find the puns in certain titles. Research the colours that you've never heard of. Try and work out which stories are complete fabrications, which ones contain nuggets of truth, and which ones are versions of real life events.

Order from Amazon:
ISBN: 978-1-910542-13-2 (paperback)
978-1-910542-14-9 (ebook)

Chapeltown Books

Potpourri
by Anusha VR

Potpourri is an eccentric mix of stories and poems. Somewhere between working twelve hour shifts at a tax firm and cramming for exams, these stories and poems tumbled onto torn sheets and paper napkins. Potpourri is an attempt at preventing the literary world slipping away and regaining a sliver of that bookish world.

Order from Amazon:

ISBN: 978-1-910542-21-7 (paperback)
978-1-910542-22-4 (ebook)

Chapeltown Books

Badlands
by Alyson Faye

A collection of flash fiction pieces, from drabbles of 100 words to longer pieces up to 1000 words. They reflect an interest in ghost stories, history especially the Victorians, old movies, derelict buildings, real life issues such as homelessness, and just the 'what if' factor of when a seemingly normal situation starts to tilt off centre, dangerously so.

A surprising collection of creepy tales. Tales so twisted, you won't want to read them at night. I didn't, I read them in an afternoon. They are brilliant
(Amazon)

Order from Amazon:

ISBN: 978-1-910542-25-5 (paperback)
978-1-910542-26-2 (ebook)

Chapeltown Books

www.ingramcontent.com/pod-product-compliance
Lightning Source LLC
Chambersburg PA
CBHW080753120626
46557CB00005B/1257